KU-337-288

Schools Library and Information Services

S00000671270

Just Like Sisters

For Matilda, Thomasin and Beatrice.
– A.McA.
To my beloved sister Zebrina.
– S.F.

DUDLEY PUBLIC LIBRARIES

L 47975

671270 | SCH

JY MAC

SIMON AND SCHUSTER

First published in Great Britain in 2005 by Simon & Schuster UK Ltd

Africa House, 64-78 Kingsway, London WC2B 6AH

Text copyright © 2005 Angela McAllister

Illustrations copyright © 2005 Sophie Fatus

The right of Angela McAllister and Sophie Fatus to be identified

as the author and illustrator of this work has been asserted by them

in accordance with the Copyright, Designs and Patents Act, 1988

Book designed by Genevieve Webster

The text for this book is set in Bodoni

The illustrations are rendered in acrylics

All rights reserved, including the right of reproduction in whole or in part in any form

A CIP catalogue record for this book is available from the British Library upon request

ISBN 0-689-87311-5

Printed in China

1 3 5 7 9 10 8 6 4 2

Just Like Sisters

Angela McAllister

Sophie Fatus

SIMON AND SCHUSTER

London New York Sydney

Nancy's penfriend was coming to visit from Florida.

Nancy read all Ally's letters over again.

"We know each other so well, we're almost sisters,"

she said happily.

Ally's plane was right on time.

"Nance!" cried Ally. "You're exactly how I imagined."

She gave her a big hug.

"How was your flight?" asked Nancy's mum.

"Great!" said Ally. "They showed my favourite movie."

"We're going to be just like sisters," said Nancy.

Ally took her hand and squeezed it.

"Yes," she said, "I want to do everything that you do."

On the way back from the airport, they stopped at the pizza
parlour. Ally ate nine Spicy Shrimp pizzas and broke a chair.
"Don't worry. Mum gave me extra money for accidents," she said.

When they got home Nancy took Ally straight up to her bedroom.

"These are my treasures," she said. Ally loved them all.

Then Ally got out her photo album. "This is my brother, Snap.

He'll be so handsome when his brace comes off," she sighed.

Nancy played her favourite songs and Ally taught her
to dance the Swamp Stomp and the Crazy Creek Creep
until they both fell about laughing.
"You're wonderful, Ally," said Nancy.
"Why, yes I am!" Ally said with a grin.

Later on Dad popped his head round the door.

"Would you girls like to share the big bed?" he said.

"Mum and I can sleep in the bunks."

But Nancy and Ally were too excited to go to sleep.

They tried Mum's lipstick, watched television and

finished two tubs of ice-cream.

The next day Nancy and Ally went shopping.

They bought everything exactly the same.

"Pink suits both of us," said Ally happily. "People

might think we're twins."

Nancy took Ally to the swimming pool.

"She's my penfriend," Nancy told the girls proudly.

Ally dashed straight up to the diving board.

"Look out below!" she yelled. Then she jumped, twisted, touched her nose with her tail, did a double loop-the-loop and belly-flopped SPLASH! into the pool – giving everyone a shower!

Ally wanted to try everything.

She joined in Nancy's ballet class.

"Think of yourselves as young trees

gently waving in the breeze," said Madame.

Ally thought of herself as a tree.

"You look like a log, dear," said Madame.

But at the end of the class Ally gave

a performance all of her own.

"Now I'm an enchanted log!" she cried with a twirl.

"Magnificent!" gasped Madame.

That afternoon they went rollerskating in the park.

"This is great," cried Ally. "Look at me, I'm flying!"

And she flew straight into a bush.

Later, when all the scrapes and scratches were bandaged,

Ally gave Nancy and the girls a ride.

On Friday the girls went to the beach.

They built castles and played frisbee.

Then a boy in trouble called for help.

"I'll save you!" cried Ally, and she zoomed towards him
like a green torpedo.
When he saw Ally the boy suddenly found he could swim again,
but she rescued him anyway.

That evening Nancy and Ally made friendship

bracelets for each other.

"I'll always wear this and think of you," said Nancy.

"I don't want to go home tomorrow," said Ally.

A big teardrop rolled down her cheek. "I'll write

to you straight away on the plane."

All Ally's new friends came to see her off at the airport.

The man taking the luggage peered over his desk.

"Is your sister going too?" he asked.

Nancy and Ally beamed happily.

"Sisters are together even when they're apart," said Nancy.

"You bet!" said Ally.